THE WITCH APOTHECARY

THE OKRITH NOVELLAS
BOOK TWO

A.K. MULFORD

Paperback 978-0-473-59671-2

Ebook 978-1-923184-06-0

Publisher AK Mulford

2021

New Zealand

Cover designed by MiblArt

Map by Holly Dunn Designs

Interior Formatting by K. Elle Morrison

NORTHERN COU[RT]
Murreneir
Brufdoran
DRÜNEHAN
Vurstyn
HIGH MOUNTAIN COURT
Valkene
YEXSHIRE
SEA OF CALLIPHO
SWIFTHILL
WESTERN COURT
Silver Sands Harbor
OKRITH

N
...port
SEA OF WETAMUIR
Falhampton
ROTTED PEAK
EASTERN COURT
WYNREACH
Haaskmouth
SOUTHERN COURT
Crushwold
SAXBRIDGE

CHAPTER ONE

Tall grasses swished at her legs. Heather stood stock still, staring out at the field as tendrils of her copper hair whipped across her face, escaping from her tight braids. A train of colorful wagons parked in a spiraling circle in the distance.

The *Carnivale du Fareas*.

It was the most famous traveling carnival in all of Okrith. Unhitched horses grazed in the fields beyond the fairground, signaling that the wagons weren't just passing through. Heather couldn't believe they had stopped in their little town. She wondered if they had come for the harvest moon celebrations. She wasn't the only person mesmerized by the new arrivals. Humans and witches alike meandered through the caravan of rickety wagons, peering with excitement into each open window.

Glancing back over her shoulder, Heather's eyes followed the forest trail to the town of Valtene. She squeezed the wicker handle of the foraging basket in her hands. She had promised her father that she would fill it with fennel before dinnertime. Brown witches always needed more fennel, and it was still growing heartily at the eastern edge of the forest, despite the autumnal frosts.

Every day was spent foraging, grinding herbs, and making potions. She hadn't ever traveled from Valtene, and, as the eldest child, she was expected to remain. Looking out over the fairground, she released a soft sigh. If she couldn't go out into the world, at least the world could come to her. Wagons carrying goods from every corner of Okrith waited downhill from where she stood. Her fingers tingled, itching to go explore.

Heather frowned at the basket in her hand. She would grab a quick handful of fennel on the way home and say it was all she could find. Decision made, she jogged through the tall grasses toward the carnival witches unloading their wares.

Each of the wagons was painted in a rainbow of hues with whorls of gold, a unique pattern on each. A burly man carried a roll of carpet over his shoulder, his waxed mustache absurdly curled. A woman wore a belt dripping with colorful glass beads and bells that jingled as she walked. Heather suddenly felt plain in her cinnamon-brown cloak, her copper hair bound in two neat braids that hung over her shoulders.

She paused at a table of jewelry. On it sat ribbon bracelets in the patron colors of the five witch covens: red, blue, brown, green, and violet. Heather's fingers lingered over the brown one, almost bronze. Her coven had the least exciting color. She knew it was meant to represent the earth, the bark of the trees, and other healing magics, but violet was more exciting. Of course, the violet witch coven had disappeared nearly a century ago. Only four covens remained in Okrith now.

"Are you buying or browsing?" a gruff witch asked as he

hoisted a large crate out of the back of his wagon. The witches were easy to spot, even the ones from out of town, because most witches wore their totem bags around their necks. The small black pouches held trinkets of personal significance, imbued with moonlight blessings each full moon. Heather kept hers tucked into the neckline of her dress, to keep from bouncing around, but the black strings could be seen easily enough. If someone needed a witch healer, they could identify her.

"Just looking," Heather murmured, her cheeks heating as she moved her fingers away from the bracelets.

"Then go look somewhere else," he said, tipping his head to the next wagon. His eyes flashed blue for a split second, revealing him as a member of the blue witch coven.

As she ambled off, she stole one more look at the witch setting down his heavy crate, its contents clinking. She wondered if he was a fortune teller. Blue witches had the gift of Sight. Most of the powerful blue witches served the royal fae, but oracles and fortune tellers made good coin as well.

Before her head spun around to see where she was going, her hip bumped into the rickety wood table set out in front of the next wagon.

Someone snorted from inside. "Definitely not a blue witch, then. I'm guessing brown." A head peeked out from the window above her. "Was I right?"

Heather's heart hammered in her chest as she looked up at the witch leaning casually on the sill above her. She had tawny brown skin and black hair cropped close to the scalp, apart from the few midnight curls allowed to grow at the top of her head. Her golden brown eyes and full lips danced with held-back laugher, her muscled frame taking up the whole window. Heather had never seen anyone like her before. She was built like a knight with the face of a goddess. The witch cocked her head at Heather, her cheeks dimpling as Heather gaped.

Heather's eyes snapped back down, breaking the spell. "Yes, I'm a brown witch," she said. "An obvious conclusion, considering we're in Valtene."

The witch above her huffed and moved to the back of the wagon.

"Guess what kind I am," the witch said with a smirk.

Heather rolled her eyes. "I don't know . . . green?"

The witch cackled, her voice deep and raspy. "Does it look like I bake cakes and grow plants?"

Biting her lip, Heather shook her head. She didn't know what this witch looked like, but she couldn't stop staring.

"Shall I show you?" The witch smiled, her eyes filling with a crimson glow, magical red flames licking up her arms. A wooden crate from inside the wagon floated out on the air and set itself gently on the ground. The witch climbed down after it with the stealth of a mountain lion.

"You're a red witch," Heather breathed, hypnotized by the red glow in her eyes. The witch blinked, and her eyes returned to their warm brown.

"Is that surprising?" She leaned forward, resting her corded forearms on the table between them. Heather's eyes snagged on the straining muscles stretching the witch's short-sleeved tunic.

"No, I . . . ," Heather said, flustered. "I've just never met a red witch before. You usually keep to yourselves."

"Ah well, the Temple of Yexshire was not for me." The witch shrugged, as if what she was saying were not a big deal. The witches were free to go anywhere in the realm, but many liked to stay in their own courts with their own traditions unless they were hired out by a rich fae. The brown witches would accept patronage from most high-class families, but the red witches refused to serve anyone other than the High Mountain fae. The red coven was esteemed above all others. It wasn't their powers of levitation that set them above the rest, it was the reverence that the High Mountain fae held for them. The High Mountain Court knew the value of their witches and it made all of Okrith value them too.

"How long have you been a part of *Carnivale du Fareas*?" Heather wondered, peering up at the midnight blue wagon, a golden sun painted on its side.

"A couple years."

"Must be lonely."

The red witch shrugged. "We're a tight-knit bunch."

"Is it hard always being on the road?" Heather asked, trying to keep the conversation going. She eyed the high canvas roof of the wagon with envy. To live in a home that could travel the realm seemed so magical.

"We circle Okrith every few years, but we're not always on the move. We're heading down to Saxbridge for the winter months. We'll be in residence there for a long while."

"I've always wanted to see Saxbridge." Heather stared wistfully to the horizon, conjuring an image in her mind of what the Southern Court capital looked like. They said the city was built of white marble, with exotic gardens and incredible foods. People wore colors of every shade of the rainbow. Heather frowned down at her plain cream-colored dress. "Is it as incredible as they say?"

"More so." The witch reached out and rubbed Heather's braid between her thumb and forefinger, snapping Heather's gaze back to hers. "What is your name?"

"Heather." Her pulse hammered in her throat.

"Pleased to meet you, Heather. I'm Emry," she said, watching Heather from hooded eyes.

The buzz of magic around Emry's aura was so strong Heather could feel it even when she wasn't glowing. Everything about the red witch seemed otherworldly and magnificent. The brown witches were respected for their medicinal remedies and healing aids, but they were still seen as the servants of the fae. There was nothing exciting or glamorous about them. With their scarlet cloaks and air of importance, every witch wanted to be a red witch.

Heather was certain she should say goodbye now. What more conversation could she carry on with this strange, beautiful witch? But her feet remained planted firmly on the spot.

Emry's cheeks dimpled as she held Heather's gaze. "I could use another pair of hands unpacking . . . if you have some time to spare?"

Heather pressed her lips together, knowing the red witch would get along fine without her help. "I don't know, I'm pretty clumsy, but I can try."

Curse the Moon. She sounded like such a bumbling fool.

"You'll do fine," Emry said, turning to the crate behind her and unfastening the latch. Opening the lid, she fished out a skein of colorful sparkling ribbons and passed it to Heather. "Here, you can do the garlands. I don't have much of an eye for decorating."

Heather snorted. "Nor I, but I will do my best."

Emry unpacked the crate as Heather unwound the ribbon. They fell into easy conversation, the stilted manner of their greeting melting into flowing banter about their favorite fairy tales and foods. A green witch came past from the center of the spiral and offered them some freshly baked biscuits. They ate, sharing a skin of water between them and leaning against the spokes of the wagon wheel. Emry smelled like the forest after rainfall. Her dimples were mesmerizing, her eyes like liquid bronze. Holding her gaze felt like standing at the edge of a cliff, exhilarating and terrifying all at once.

Heather couldn't keep track of how they flitted from one topic to the next, practically stumbling over each other with excitement as they spoke. Every time Emry laughed at Heather's jokes, she felt like she grew an inch taller, suddenly taking up more space in the world. Each grin and chuckle made her desperate to find another anecdote that would make the red witch smile.

In those few brief moments, Heather felt like she knew more about Emry than anyone she had ever known. Emry's favorite season was autumn in the Eastern Kingdom, her favorite animal was the High Mountain hawk, and she was deathly afraid of bats.

"The worst animal for a witch to fear," Heather said, chuckling as she unspooled the last bit of ribbon from the skein with deliberate slowness. It had taken her the better part of three hours to cover the stall from that single roll, afraid that if it finished, she wouldn't have an excuse to stay any longer.

"I hide it well." Emry smirked, her warm eyes roving Heather's face. "Don't go telling everyone."

"I'll keep your secret," Heather murmured, watching as Emry's gaze dropped to her hands, a secret smile playing across her face.

"I still can't believe you prefer the scent of lavender to blooming amethyst," Emry teased, setting out three chunky white candles in the center of her table.

Heather eyed the candles, then glanced up at the sky.

The sun was far below the tree line, and long shadows had grown all around them.

"Mother Moon," Heather cursed. "I should have left hours ago. My mother's going to kill me."

She dropped the remaining ribbon on the table. The hours had slipped through her fingers like water, feeling like she'd arrived just moments ago. Her mind scrambled for excuses to stay as Emry placed a gentle hand on the crook of Heather's arm, snapping Heather's mind back to the red witch in front of her.

"Thank you for helping me set up my shop," Emry said. "It was far more fun than I would have had alone."

"I had fun too." Heather felt the blush creeping up her neck as Emry reached out and brushed Heather's copper braid over her shoulder.

"You should come see the carnival when it's open tomorrow. It is truly magical." Emry spoke with such casualness, but Heather hoped she knew what Emry was really asking: will I see you again?

"Yes, I know my siblings will be eager to come," she said, holding her hands tightly in front of herself to keep from fidgeting. "I will . . . um . . . see you tomorrow."

She tried not to cringe, certain she sounded like an idiot.

"I'll see you tomorrow, Heather." Emry's eyes danced as she said her name. Heather felt every syllable skitter across her body like a whisper.

She hastened back the way she came, her face still burning, hoping the red witch was still watching her go.

The skies grayed as nighttime descended. Pinpricks of evening rain dotted the ground. Heather ambled along the forest path, toying with her braids, remembering the way that red witch had touched it. Emry. Heather tossed her name around in her mind. She felt like she knew Emry as well as any lifelong friend. They had a word for it in Mhenbic, the witch's native tongue: *hidaraast*. It meant the eerie familiarity of a new thing. Heather was certain she had never met Emry before, but her mind kept combing back through her life, trying to pinpoint how she seemed to know Emry so well.

Carnivale du Fareas would be in town another few days, until the harvest moon, and then they would be disappearing south. Heather already knew she would head back to the carnival the next day after work. Her empty fingers skimmed the outstretched branches, her other hand clutching the basket of sleeping thistle, a weed used as a calming aid. She didn't have time to circle back to the eastern part of the forest for the fennel. She could use it as her excuse to go back to the fair in the coming days.

A crack of thunder sounded overhead. Heather ran the rest of the distance to the main road, a few other stragglers darting indoors before the deluge. Holding the handful of fuzzy broad leaves over her head as a shield, Heather dashed into the third storefront on the left, narrowly escaping the heavy patter of rain that followed her into the door.

The string of bells above her tinkled as she entered under the sign reading Doledir Apothecary.

Her father looked up from his ledger, adjusting his golden spectacles. "You're late. We've already had supper," he said. He was not angry, only weary. The long hours of running the village apothecary were draining.

Heather was old enough to help run the place, though she did a terrible job of it. She had clumsy hands, always dropping the glass vials. She swore they should all be wrapped in linen. Being the eldest child of the Doledir family, one day she would take over the brown witch shop, so it was time to start taking her apprenticeship more seriously.

"Shall I lock up?" Heather asked her father, blowing out the candle by the window.

Her father simply nodded, removing his spectacles to rub his tired eyes. His wheezing breath rattled in his throat. He had been poorly for most of Heather's life. No amount of brown witch magic seemed to cure his rasping breaths and pallid coloring.

Heather snicked the lock and bolted the door, flipping over the sign to announce to all that the store was closed. The rain poured down outside the stained glass window. Soon that rain would be turning to snow, the harvest moon signaling the change of season for the witches. They celebrated the solstices and equinoxes, but the moons were the life cycle of their religion, the Moon Goddess the only deity the witches prayed to.

Heather meandered over to the workbench. Baskets of dried herbs and mushrooms dotted the surface, each with little paper cards displaying their names and medicinal properties. While there were many brown witches in the town of Valtene, most of the residents were humans, and humans couldn't tell the difference between a medicinal mushroom and a poisonous one. The Doledir witches made a good albeit modest living from the humans' ineptitude regarding medicinal plants.

She moved to the next table to cover the baskets of aromatic herbs with a cloth, only to find them already done.

"I finished your chores while you were out foraging," a nasally voice said as Heather's little sister popped up from where she was tidying baskets beneath the tables.

Two years younger, Rose wasn't so little. She was already a head taller than Heather with a mop of blonde hair, a lanky frame, and deep ocean blue eyes. Rose was sullen but fastidious, a diligent worker with a sharp mind who never forgot a task. She was already more help running the family business than Heather. Heather was certain her parents regretted that Rose hadn't been born first. Even if Heather inherited the apothecary in name, Rose would be the one to run it.

Rose frowned at the measly bundle of herbs in Heather's hand. "What is that?"

Grabbing a coil of twine, Heather snipped off a length with the scissors resting on the window ledge. "Sleeping thistle." She wound the twine around the stems, knotting the bunch together.

"Oh good." Her father closed his ledger and dusted his ink-stained hands on the front of his vest. "Mrs. Hawkins has been buying us out of our calming balms this season."

"You were meant to be getting fennel," Rose said, eyeing the empty basket in Heather's hand.

Heather glared at her sister. She could be such a little rat.

"There was none left in the eastern corner," she lied. "The frosts must have gotten them. I will check the western side of the Wyxshire Wood tomorrow."

"Mm." Rose rolled her eyes, dramatically folding her arms as she crossed the room and stomped up the back stairs.

Rose and her attitude. She was as grim as they came. Heather huffed, tying the bundle of herbs on the line of rope hanging in the front window. The herbs dried the quickest there. It had the sunniest prospect and was close enough to the fireplace for the rainy days.

Heather snorted, thinking of poor Mrs. Hawkins while she hung the sleeping thistle. "I don't think any amount of magic will keep her calm while she's still married to that philandering husband of hers," she muttered.

"Heather," her father scolded, though there was laughter in his voice. "A shop owner cannot say such things. Confidentiality is tantamount."

"No one is here but you and me."

"Yes, but better to not," her father insisted, covering his mouth to cough.

Valtene was a medium-sized town on the border of the Western and Northern Courts, but they gossiped like it was a village of ten families.

Heather turned back to her father. "Do you want me to dust?"

"No, that's quite alright," he said, moving over to her and giving her a tired hug like he did most evenings before bed. "Go eat. Your Ma left out a bowl and some bread. Just wash up after—we don't need any more mice."

Heather bobbed her chin, making her way to the back of the shop and through the heavy velvet curtains that led to their kitchen. Sure enough, a bowl of cold stew and a hunk of bread sat covered by a dishcloth on the dining table. Bringing a candle from the mantle over to the table, Heather sat and ate in silence. It was pleasant to have a meal without the usual clamor of her four loud siblings and bantering parents.

Footsteps thundered overhead.

Her life was joyful chaos. Chatter echoed down the back stairwell and Evelyn came rushing out to the table,

Oliver right behind her. They wore their long white night-shirts, ready for bed. The season had grown cold enough for them to wear their long-sleeved garments now.

"Did you see the carnival?" Evelyn prodded, brushing her long mane of auburn hair over her shoulder.

"Will you take us tomorrow?" Oliver added eagerly, his blue eyes the size of saucers.

Heather swallowed her mouthful of stew and shook her head. "I was out foraging today."

"A likely story," tittered a voice from the stairwell as her ma turned the corner. Her white apron was still perfectly starched and clean, despite the fact it was the end of the day. The wisps of flaxen hair that broke free from the bun at the nape of her neck were the only testament to the business of the day.

"I brought back sleeping thistle," Heather said, biting into a chunk of bread and making a note to put the dough into the proofing baskets before bed. She was in charge of making the morning loaves for the family and was meant to put them in at lunchtime. The dough would probably not be as airy and leavened as usual.

"You mean the sleeping thistle that is growing like a weed all through the path to the fairgrounds?" Her mother arched her thin brow, giving Heather a knowing look.

Heather's cheeks heated. "I may have had a peek."

Her siblings erupted into questions at that: how many caravans, what did the people look like, what sort of games did they have, and most importantly, would she take them tomorrow?

Her mother laughed. Lifting the brush in her hand back to Evelyn's hair, she brushed and listened as her younger children kept up a chorus of "please?".

"I'll take you tomorrow if it is okay with Ma," Heather said, her siblings' eyes instantly darting to their mother.

Ma chuckled, putting the brush back in her pocket and beginning to plait Evelyn's hair for sleep. Their mother braided each of her daughters' hair every night before bed. It kept their hair from tangling, but it was also an act of love, each one of them getting that moment in time to chat with their mother about their day before bed. Heather was eighteen now, but she still let her mother do it. She cherished that time when she had her mother's full attention. It was a rare moment in the day indeed.

Her siblings waited with bated breath until her mother said, "Once you finish your chores, you may go."

Evelyn and Oliver erupted into giddy cheers. They were the youngest of Heather's siblings, eight and ten years old. The older two, Rose and Cole, were probably still upstairs reading their books before bed, nonplussed about the famous carnival being in town. Rose was the most level-headed person Heather knew. She was the last person to be bewitched by a traveling carnival.

"Come on you two, let's say our prayers to Mother Moon," Ma said, steering her youngest offspring back up the stairs.

A mewling sound came from below the table before Heather felt the soft brush of a cat winding between her legs. She plucked a piece of beef from her stew and dropped it onto the floor, looking down at Raven.

"You are meant to be catching mice," Heather whispered to the black cat, its gold and green eyes peering up at her. Raven purred loudly, headbutting Heather's legs again. "Fine," she said, scooping up the cat with a hand under its belly and plonking it into her lap.

Raven was meant to be the shop cat. Ma had found her

as a kitten, abandoned in the woods. Heather had been six years old at the time, and Raven still hadn't learned to scare away the mice.

Raven pawed at Heather's hand in a bid for more beef as Heather's mind wandered back to Emry. Heather planned to wear her hair back in a single, loose braid tomorrow. It would make her look more sophisticated. The two braids made her seem too childish. She wondered what Emry would think if she rouged her cheeks and painted her lips. She knew it shouldn't matter one bit what the red witch thought of her. She would be gone in a few days.

CHAPTER TWO

The fairground was transformed into a magical realm of fire dancers and soothsayers, with rows of goods from every corner of the Okrith, the air filled with the scent of honey wine and hickory smoke. The legion of wagons had arranged themselves in a mystical spiral, leading the visitors round and round, circling farther and farther into the *Carnivale du Fareas'* enchanting depths.

Tassels blowing in the breeze, Heather pulled her knit wool shawl tighter around her shoulders. The shadows were already growing long in the early afternoon. Evelyn and Oliver bounced back and forth between the narrow rows of tables, Evelyn's candied apple already eaten down to the core. Heather's eyes roved the stalls: goat leather for binding spellbooks, sparkling crystals of every hue, elaborate totem bags embroidered with gold a seamstress waiting to personalize each bag with a witch's name. Pausing, Heather looked down at the plain black pouch on her chest. She supposed it would be beneficial to know which one was hers . . . especially with four other siblings, but then she saw the card that read "personalization: 15 *druni*" and she kept walking.

They passed the fortune teller from the day before. He was resplendent in a fuchsia jacket that shimmered under the flickering torchlight, a long black feather trailing from his silver toque. A giant yellow snake wrapped his shoulders, its tongue testing the air. The three Doledir siblings gasped in unison. Heather had heard of these creatures from the far south, but she had never seen one before.

"You can give her a pat if you like," the blue witch called, his eyes glowing a dazzling cerulean. Evelyn and Heather shook their heads at once, but brave young Oliver advanced a step. "Like this," the witch said, softly running his fingers down toward the snake's tail.

"It won't bite me?" Oliver asked, hand already suspended in the air to touch the tail constricting the blue witch's arm.

"She is a gentle one." The witch let out a chuckle that shook his large belly. Running a finger under the snake's chin, he added, "Aren't you, *mea raga?*"

Oliver stroked steadily down the snake's tail. "It's not slimy!" he exclaimed, whirling to Evelyn, who then stepped forward to touch the snake.

The blue witch guffawed. "A common misconception."

"You should touch it, Heather, its smooth!" Evelyn said.

Heather shook her head, pulling her shawl tighter around her. "I will not be touching one of those, thank you."

"What about one of these?" a low voice sounded behind her.

Heather whipped her head around, already knowing who spoke. Emry stood there in her carnival garb: a burgundy tunic with silver and gold filigree that showed off her broad shoulders and muscular arms. Gold leaf dusted her short black hair, and thick smudges of kohl lined her angular eyes. She was a mythical being, like a painting from a fairy tale, so unreal that Heather gaped at her for a long while, not noticing the bird perched in her hand.

Oliver pushed forward. "Is that your bird? Is it a crow?"

"It's a raven," Emry replied, looking down at the boy, eyes crinkling with amusement. "And hi, I'm Emry."

Oliver quickly made his introductions, having forgotten himself in the excitement of seeing the bird. They did not have ravens in the west; they were native to the Eastern slopes.

"We have a cat named Raven," Evelyn added.

"Excellent choice," Emry said, giving Heather a wink that caused Heather's heart to stutter.

Emry was so sure of herself, like she was gliding over water, whereas Heather moved like a floundering fawn.

"What is your raven's name?" Heather finally said, her voice coming out an octave higher than she intended.

Emry grinned. "Raven."

"You named your raven Raven?" Oliver said incredulously. "That's a terrible name."

Heather pinched his shoulder.

"Ouch!" he exclaimed, glowering back at her.

"But good enough for a cat, I see?" Emry said, casting those kohl-lined eyes down to Heather's little brother. Emry kissed the head of the sleek black bird, causing its head to bob up. Its iridescent wings shimmered under the fading light. "I call him Ravi for short."

"Can we touch him too?" Oliver prodded.

Emry nodded. "Like this," she said, smoothing a flat hand from Ravi's shoulders down toward his tail feathers. She lowered the bird for Oliver to reach.

The raven let out a sharp, booming caw as Oliver

stroked his feathers, and Oliver yanked his hand back, causing the rest of them to burst into laughter.

"It's the problem with pet ravens," Emry said with a smirk, stroking Ravi's back again. "They are a noisy bunch."

She turned to her table of wares and put the raven on a perch beside her stall. An attendant scurried past them, lighting the torches that dotted the path, preparing for nightfall.

"He won't fly off?" Evelyn asked.

"I found Ravi as a fledgling," Emry said, shaking her head. "He has one malformed wing. He can't fly . . . though he does like riding at the front of the wagon when we travel. I think he likes the feeling of the wind in his feathers."

Lips twisting up, Heather assessed Emry again. She felt pulled under by whatever spell the red witch had cast on her the moment she touched her braid the day before. Emry turned to Heather with a grin, and Heather dropped her gaze, pressing her lips tightly together as she was caught staring.

"You want a tour of the fair?" Emry offered to Heather's siblings.

"Yes!" they eagerly replied at once.

"Let's go," Emry said, gesturing to the curving path.

"What about your table?" Heather nodded to Emry's stall.

The once empty table was now laden with jars of colorful spices and baskets of dried herbs. Heather eyed the small container behind some dried white flowers: bloodbane. It grew in the west, many brown witches using it in their more powerful potions and elixirs. Her great-grandmother was famous for mixing it with hellebore to make the strongest pain tonic known to magic. It was a dangerous plant, killing a person as easily as it could heal them.

"Ravi will watch the table," Emry said, eyeing the stall filled with shelves of medicinal plants and tropical spices. She gave Oliver a wicked grin. "He'll peck out the eyes of anyone who tries to pilfer while we're gone."

Oliver's eyes widened, and Heather squeezed her brother's shoulder in reassurance that the red witch was, in fact, joking.

"He seems like a very helpful assistant," Heather said, following as Emry steered their group back into the fray of fairground visitors.

"That he is," Emry said, watching Heather's siblings dart off ahead, eager not to miss a single stall. "You certainly have your hands full as the older sister of those two."

"Indeed." Heather chortled. "And there's two more between me and them, too. They're still back at the house." Emry's eyebrows shot up. "You don't have any siblings?"

"None." Emry shook her head.

"And your parents?" Heather regretted prying the second she said it, turning her gaze to a table of light catchers. Strings of colored glass beads sent fractals of light dancing across the stall. The Doledirs had a modest version of one hanging up in the window of the apothecary, but it was a simple string with three cloudy glass beads, nothing like these long rainbow strings, designed to draw the eye of patrons to their witch shops. They were also said to please the Fates and bring them good luck.

"My parents still live in the Temple of Yexshire along with most of the red witch coven," Emry said, puffing out her chest. "They, of course, disapprove of my nomadic lifestyle."

"I have never met a red witch before." Heather's cheeks dimpled. "Are they all like you?"

Those golden brown eyes slid back to Heather. "What

am I like?" Emry asked softly, her voice falling into a low murmur that made the hairs on Heather's arms stand on end. She could listen to that sound all night.

"I don't know," Heather hedged, busying her hands at the table of crystals, her fingers running over a tray of sparkling yellow stones. "Enchanting," she murmured.

Blush burning up her neck, Heather heard the soft huff of Emry's laughter as the red witch stepped up to the table beside her, her burgundy tunic brushing the sleeve of Heather's dress. The contact was electrifying.

"Citrine," Emry said, her hands beginning to glow crimson. One of the tiny yellow stones lifted into the air and hovered in front of them, making Heather gasp. "A good choice. It will keep the sunshine with you in the dark months ahead."

Heather shook her head. "I can't afford it. I will just have to imagine the sunshine."

Emry's lips jutted to the side, and the crystal floated back down onto the tray. "You could always do what I do."

"What is that?"

"Head south for the winter."

"Like a migratory bird." Heather laughed, brushing a wisp of loose hair behind her ear. Her heartbeat was louder than the sound of flapping pennants and the faint cheers of revelers that echoed around her. "I'm afraid I can't load my apothecary shop onto the back of the wagon like you."

"Well if you know of any skilled brown witches," Emry said, nudging her shoulder into Heather, "I am looking to hire."

"Why?" Heather furrowed her brow.

"You've seen my stall. I buy and trade in spices and herbs and carry them throughout Okrith." Emry tipped her head back toward the way they'd come, gold dust falling from her hair. "But I could charge much more if I had a brown witch turn them into potions and elixirs."

"You carry some pretty potent things in your stall," Heather said, nibbling her bottom lip.

"You see?" Emry said, moving back down the path, the void between them instantly unbearable. Heather hustled back to her side. "You could be foraging through the jungles and the ice lakes and the stormy seasides if you came with me."

Heather's pulse ratcheted upward at the thought of just her and Emry on the road, living in the wagon and traveling throughout the realm. Her mind toppled into the fantasy, so easy to imagine, but it was a daydream and nothing more. She had a family to help look after. She couldn't just up and leave.

The path opened up as they entered the center of the spiral, but a horde of people crammed into the circular space. A crowd of merry witches danced, their ceremonial brooms draped with golden bells that provided a chorus of tinkling every time the group jumped and swayed. The brooms were a symbol of the harvest moon, a time to ready for the winter and prepare for leaner months, to clean out the stores before the snow fell.

Heather's gaze was drawn upward. Two giant poles rose into the air, acrobats dancing with their brooms on a rope strung between them. It was a fantastical celebration, nothing like how their family normally celebrated the harvest moon. The Doledirs just laid the shop broom on the floor, each of them jumping over the broomstick and making a wish to get them through the winter, then heading to the graveyard to pray to their ancestors. The witches celebrated with the spirits of their families, but it was nothing like this wild revelry.

The drinks flowed freely, many of the patrons holding mugs of hot cider or goblets of wine from the stalls lining the center of the spiral. Heather eyed the rows of colorful sweets and bubbling cauldrons of festive beverages.

"Have you ever had one of these?" Emry asked, picking up a powdered cake from a tray. She nodded to the stall owner, a portly gray-haired witch, who nodded back in seeming acknowledgement that Emry was taking the food.

"I have no idea what that is." Heather bit her cheek as she took the little cake Emry passed her.

"Try it," Emry urged with a grin.

The sweetness of sugar melting on her tongue was quickly followed by a bright burst of spice—cinnamon and nutmeg and the savory smoothness of pumpkin. Heather hummed, closing her eyes to relish the flavors. When she opened them again, Emry was staring at her, lips parted, eyes filled with a molten heat that sent tingles from the tip of Heather's head into her toes.

A loud squawking sound snapped their eyes from that magnetizing hold.

"It's Ravi," Emry grumbled. "I guess I have customers." She took a step away from Heather but then turned back, as if she were warring with herself over whether she should go. "Will you come back tomorrow?"

The eagerness in Emry's voice made Heather's stomach flip. Heather gave the barest of nods, still spelled by the wanton look that had crossed the red witch's face.

"Good," Emry said with a grin that made every other carnival excitement fade into the background. "Have fun." And with that she turned. Heather's eyes tracked her until she disappeared into the crowd.

Wyxshire Wood was quiet midweek. Patches of forest remained in brilliant greens while others were in full autumnal bloom, yielding to the cooler weather. Most of the townsfolk had already absconded to the *Carnivale du Fareas*. But Rose and Heather were left behind to forage with their father. The Doledirs knew the best secret spots off the worn paths where all sorts of mystical Western plants grew. They could spot them as easily as they could identify letters and numbers, the brown witches priding themselves on their plant knowledge.

Apron laden with herbs, Heather leaned against a tree to catch her breath. The canopy cast cool shadows upon them as she took a deep breath of fresh air.

"You should tie those up now before you crush all the leaves," Rose instructed as she dutifully wrapped the parcel of witch's sorrel in string and hung it from her belt. A skirt of foraged bundles ringed Rose's waist, her systems always the most efficient. Heather would have to spend hours sorting her foraged greens and flowers when they returned to the shop. She had to be careful not to leave a flower that inflamed passions amongst herbs that cured toothaches . . . again.

"She's right," their father called from up ahead, a wide wicker basket of mushrooms in his hand.

Heather gritted her teeth. Rose was always right. Her sister was clever and cunning, if a little cold.

"If Rose is so good at this, why don't just the two of you come? I could stay back at the shop," Heather groused, moving toward the vine of stinging sallow twining its way up an oak tree.

"You would destroy an entire display shelf if we left you there alone," Rose said, wiping her sweaty brow with the back of her hand.

"That was one time," Heather growled.

"You are still more helpful to us than not," her father said mildly, muffling a cough as he continued to pluck mushrooms from the rotten log at his feet.

"Thanks," Heather said, taking out the knife from her belt. She held the vine through a cloth so as not to sting her fingers and began slicing it into short sticks. This weekly trip into the forest had been particularly fruitful. It was a good thing too, since winter would be upon them soon and the forest would go to sleep under a blanket of snow. There would be no foraging apart from the occasional winter berry.

"You could just try harder, is all," Rose added, making Heather clench her jaw. She was already trying much harder than she would like to be.

"Maybe I'm not cut out for the apothecary business," Heather finally said. "Maybe I shall go apprentice the baker or seamstress and Rose can take over the shop."

"Don't be ridiculous," her father tutted, adjusting his fogged spectacles. "You are the eldest. You are born with the strongest magic, so you are given the privilege of inheriting the family legacy. Be grateful for it. There are children begging on the street."

Oh yes, the begging children. They always got brought up when her father needed to make a point.

"You don't just abandon your family," Rose said as she bundled another handful of sorrel, having nearly picked the forest clean. They always left some behind. It was a witch rule to never take it all. Not only so that it would regrow, but also to respect the spirits of the forest. The Goddess in the moon looked down on all living things and demanded her forests be treated with respect.

"I'm not abandoning anyone," Heather sighed, pulling twine from her back pocket and starting to wrap the lengths of sallow.

A cough from the far left had them all whirling. A confident figure stood there, short hair tousling in the breeze. Her charcoal wool coat bulked out her frame as she tucked her hands into her trouser pockets.

Emry.

"Sorry to interrupt," Emry said, smirking up at them, her eyes snagging on Heather.

"Yes?" Heather's father straightened, clearly surprised that someone had found them so far off the trail.

"Apologies," Emry said again. "I was looking for the owner of Doledir Apothecary. The shop was closed, and the farrier said you were out foraging."

"And you managed to follow our trail?" Heather asked, chewing nervously at her lip.

Emry cocked her head at Heather in a way that made Heather want to hold her breath.

"You weren't trying to hide your trail, were you?" Emry said, letting out a deep chuckle. "If so, I think I should teach you some tricks to better go undetected."

Heather almost accepted the offer right then and there. She would love for Emry to teach her how to sneak around in the woods, just the two of them. The thought of being alone with the red witch made her heart thump so loudly she wondered if the others could hear it.

"No, it is fine," Heather's father said. "I am Mr. Doledir. What can I do for you?"

"I am a stall keeper from the *Carnivale du Fareas.*" Emry straightened her shoulders, so at home in every space she took up. That charisma was magnetizing. "I trade in herbs and spices from all over."

"We don't buy foreign herbs," her father rasped. "Our remedies are made only from Western plants." He said it like it was a point of pride.

"I do not wish to sell." Emry's cheeks dimpled in a delicious way. Heather peeked at Rose, who looked down at the red witch with cool indifference. Her sister was clearly not under the red witch's spell like Heather. "I am looking to buy out some of your stock to take down to Saxbridge."

"We usually don't sell to traders," her father hedged. "How much are you looking at buying?"

"500 *druni*'s worth," Emry replied, making Heather's mouth drop open. 500 *druni* was more than they would make all winter.

"What stock are you looking for?" Rose asked warily. "We might not have that much of what you need."

"Well that is why I was planning on visiting you at your shop and not in the middle of the woods." Emry spoke directly to Rose, as if knowing she was the true authority behind their business. "It would be much easier to ascertain."

"Do you have the money on you now?" Rose scanned Emry's thick woolen coat.

"Why?" Emry huffed, brushing the short curls off her forehead. "Are you going to rob me?"

"She didn't mean it like that," Heather said, finally finding the ability to speak. "Besides, no one would dare cross a red witch."

Rose gasped. "You're a red witch?"

Heather's father took a few notable steps closer to Rose, as if preparing to protect his daughter from red witch magic.

"I am indeed," Emry said, eyes flickering with glowing red light at her command. The beaming scarlet rays were even more stunning in the shadows of the woods. It was the most beautiful magic Heather had ever seen. Her brown magic paled in comparison to that brilliant crimson light.

"We can take you to the shop to see for yourself," Heather's father said in a slow, nervous voice. He was probably thinking of all the havoc a red witch could wreak on their little shop of delicate glass vials.

"I'll take her," Heather interjected, ears burning at the eagerness in her voice. She took a breath and added, "There is still much to gather in the forest and only weeks until the snow comes. Like you said, Rose is better at the foraging and I am the future owner of the shop . . . I can handle this trade."

Her father's eyebrows shot up, apparently impressed by her offer. Little did he know it was not as selfless as it seemed.

Emry gestured back toward the path. "Shall we then?"

A small thrill ran through Heather's body as the glowing in those eyes ebbed, turning their full attention to her. Bobbing her chin, Heather crunched her way through the thick layer of fallen leaves, keeping pace at Emry's side.

"See you in an hour," her father called after her, but Heather just lifted a hand to him without turning. All of her attention was focused solely on the red witch walking beside her.

CHAPTER THREE

They walked in silence for several minutes, a playful smirk stretching across Emry's face. What could Heather say to her? She had no idea how to make small talk with someone who looked like Emry. Finally, she thought of something.

"Is Ravi guarding your stall?" Heather asked, her voice wobblier than she expected, making her cough to cover it.

"He's watching over the wagon," Emry said, peeking down at Heather as they wound their way along the worn forest trail. "I haven't opened up the stall for the day yet. I will this evening, but I wanted to get some supplies in town first."

"I imagine you need to restock in every town you stop in," Heather said, brushing a stray lock of hair behind her ear.

"Some towns have more than others." Emry plucked a golden leaf from a branch beside her and twirled the stem in her hand. "Valtene is larger than I thought it would be. You have many good shops. There's beautiful pottery and bead-work in the west. I even got this jacket just this morning,"

She waved her hand down the pristine wool of her new coat. It looked like Eastern Court sheep's wool, known for wicking away moisture and being hardy under constant wear.

"It suits you," Heather whispered, looking over the perfectly tailored garment, making Emry smile. Heather cleared her throat again. "Though I don't expect you will need it in Saxbridge."

Emry guffawed. "That's true, but we'll only be there for the winter and then we'll head east again, circling the continent, and a warm coat will be a wanted blessing."

"Well, you picked a fine one." Heather held her hands together nervously as the forest opened up before them and the main road of shops began to appear.

Emry followed her to the front door of Doledir Apothecary, waiting while she fumbled with the key in the lock. The door opened, the bells tinkling above their heads as they stepped inside.

"Wow," Emry said, looking around the room, eyes darting from the shelves of potions to the baskets of dried flowers to the herbs hanging in the windows. "This place is huge."

"Are all apothecaries not this size?" Heather wondered.

Emry shook her head as her eyes followed the ladder leaning against the back wall, up to the two stories filled with boxes and baskets of bulk stock.

"Have you never seen another apothecary?" Emry asked, sliding her eyes to Heather.

"I've never left Valtene," she said, looking down at her hands.

"Do you wish to?"

Heather clasped her hands together under Emry's scrutiny. "Do you think I should run away and join the traveling fair?" Heather countered with a coy smile, despite her flaming cheeks. She was sure her brown magic was glowing from her eyes now, the faint buzzing of magic pulsing out of her as it did during all heightened emotions.

"I know at least one person who would be pleased if you did." Emry pressed her plump lips together, making Heather's heart leap into her throat. "Well, two, if you count Ravi."

Heather let out a tense chortle. "How do you know Ravi would want me to come?"

"Because Ravi likes the same people I do," Emry said, picking up a vial off the shelf and inspecting it as if what she said was not a big deal at all.

But the words rocked Heather. Emry liked her. She didn't know what "like" meant, but Mother Moon, she wanted to find out. She busied her hands rearranging the baskets on the table by the window. Her mind whirled with maybes. Maybe she was misreading this whole situation. Maybe Emry liked her as a friend and nothing more. Maybe she didn't feel her heart skip a beat every time their eyes met, like Heather did.

"Is there anything in particular you were looking for?" Heather asked, ambling over to the countertop and pulling out the worn ledger, scanning the lists of inventory.

"Nettles for certain. Ipress, peat bower, and cropwood if you have it."

"We have them all," Heather said, climbing up the ladder behind the counter. She selected the large box of dried nettles. It was light as paper despite its massive size. Heather pulled it out and plonked it down onto the countertop.

Emry peered into the box from across the counter. "How much for the lot?"

"You want the whole box?" Heather pursed her lips.

"Nettles don't grow in the hot jungles of the south," Emry said.

"They are bountiful here, so we don't charge very much for them."

"Charge me more."

Heather looked up into Emry's devious eyes, that smirk playing across her face again.

"Save your money for the more expensive herbs," Heather said, trying to keep her hands from fidgeting. She couldn't stand still. Not with this gorgeous red witch looking at her.

The shop was so quiet with just the two of them. There was no hiding behind magical carnival acts and bubbling cauldrons of drinks.

Turning back to the shelf, Heather asked, "Ipress, you said? The purple or white variety?"

"Purple, if you have it. Which box is it?"

"The top right one," Heather said, arching her brow. Before she could take another step up the ladder, the box in the top right corner lifted and slowly slid itself out of its nook, floating like a feather toward the countertop.

Heather's mouth fell open as she watched the red witch's eyes glow that bright crimson, scarlet flames licking her hands. She was the most stunning creature Heather had ever seen.

As the box settled onto the countertop, Heather realized she was openly gaping. She cleared her throat. "You would come in very handy at this shop should you ever want a job. You would save me a lot of climbing."

"I'm afraid a lot of people at the carnival think the same," Emry said with a chuckle. "I help some of the older stall holders with the set up and break down of their stalls."

"Are you the only red witch in the bunch?"

"No there's two others, Ebus and Heath, though they don't have much in the way of red magic."

Heather nodded. The female witches tended to have more acute powers than the men, but there were always exceptions, like Heather's father. He was a strong brown witch. His magic infused each potion and elixir in their shop, heightening the medicinal properties of their wares.

"So the rest are what? Brown witches?"

"There's a few of everything: blue witches, brown witches, and most of the food stalls are run by green witches, of course," Emry said, watching as Heather bagged up the herbs. "There's one girl who says she's a violet witch but her magic glows blue so it's an easy lie to spot."

Heather snorted. The violet witches had all disappeared long ago. The idea of a young violet witch was laughable.

She skittered about the room, collecting the rest of the herbs Emry had requested while Emry perused the shelves. As Heather searched the cabinet by the window, she heard a soft mewling behind her. She turned to find Raven in Emry's arms, her cat purring so loudly she could hear it across the room.

"This must be your Raven." Emry laughed as Raven headbutted her chin, rubbing her midnight fur across Emry's neck.

"Yes," Heather said with a grin, placing the last of the herbs on the countertop. "Right, I think that's everything." She eyed the mountain of paper bags and boxes strewn about the countertop. "You're going to need a cart to carry all that back."

"Not if you help me carry it."

Heather's chest tightened at the offer. She wasn't ready

to say goodbye to the red witch. She hoped Emry was trying to find excuses to stay with her, too. Her father and sister wouldn't be back for another hour. She had a little time.

"Okay," she said, breathlessly.

With one more quick pat, Emry set Raven back on the floor, the black cat meowing her displeasure at being put down.

"I'll come visit again before I go," Emry said to Raven, stooping to lower her hand and Raven arching her back into Emry's palm.

"You're gone in three days," Heather said, unable to hide the sadness in her voice, fearful she was revealing too much. "Don't make promises you can't keep."

Emry's warm brown eyes glimmered in the light of the shadowed shop. "I keep my promises," she said, slowly moving over to stand beside Heather, cocking her head, assessing her with an intensity Heather had never felt before. "I'll come back to say goodbye."

Pulling her lip between her teeth, Heather's eyes dropped to the floor. "I don't want you to say goodbye."

She said it so quietly she wasn't sure if she could be heard, but a warm hand reached up and bracketed her face, pulling her gaze back up into Emry's burning one. Her heart hammered against her ribcage. Her lips parted as she took in a shallow breath. Every cell in her body homed in on that hand on her cheek, her eyes glued to the beautiful ones staring at her with all-consuming attention.

"I don't want to say goodbye either," Emry said in a low, husky voice. Her eyes dipped down to Heather's lips, making Heather's stomach clench with nerves.

Emry tipped her head down, moving so slowly, her breath skimming Heather's mouth before their lips finally met. Heather's heart leapt into her throat as those warm lips enveloped hers in a soft, slow kiss. Emry pulled away an inch, eyes scanning Heather's, an unspoken question on her face. Heather instantly responded. Lifting up on her toes, Emry's cheeks dimpled as she closed the distance between them again.

The bells on the door jangled, and the two lurched apart.

A young man wearing a crumpled brown tunic with paint-stained hands stumbled in, looking at the two of them with a grin. "Sorry to interrupt."

A vague image of him from their visit to the fair bubbled up in Heather's mind. He was one of the stall holders at the carnival. He painted caricatures of the visitors, and she remembered watching as one lady sat for her portrait.

"What do you want, Benton?" Emry snarled, making Heather blush at how badly the red witch obviously wished for that kiss to continue—as badly as Heather did herself.

"Oh, um, I was just looking for something with maybe peppermint and ginger?" The sheepish look on his face told Heather enough. He had a funny stomach and didn't want to delve into a discussion about his bowel movements with them.

"We have just the thing," Heather said, moving to the shelf of little vials on the wall. She could swear Emry's hand floated out toward her as she moved away, as if the red witch might pull Heather back to her side.

The door jangled again, and Heather's father and Rose walked back in. Heather blanched. She thought they would be gone for much longer.

"It's beginning to rain," Rose said, as if reading Heather's mind. She nodded to the mountain of herbs on the countertop. "You better double wrap those things before you carry them back to the fair."

"I was planning on it," Heather gritted out, unhappy that her sister was ordering her around. She tilted her chin to Benton. "I was just helping a customer."

"Here, I'll ring you up," Heather's father said to Emry, scuffling off to his ledger.

Heather's fingers trembled, and the small vial she'd just plucked off the shelf slid from her grasp. The instant it left her fingers she braced for the sound of shattering glass, but it didn't come. She looked down to see the vial hovering an inch above the ground. Gaping, she turned to Emry. The red witch's eyes glowed as her fingers flicked upward and the vial returned to Heather's hand.

"Wow," Heather's father said, eyebrows shooting up towards his hairline.

"We need someone like you around to make up for Heather's clumsiness," Rose said, folding her arms across her chest.

"I am the perfect companion for a clumsy witch." Emry gave Heather a wink.

Heather whirled back toward Benton as she turned the same color as Emry's glowing magic. "That'll be two coppers."

"What a bargain," he said, rummaging around his trouser pocket and producing two small copper coins. "You'd make ten times as much if you sold these in Saxbridge."

"Really?" Heather's father asked, adjusting his spectacles with a curious glance. "Those herbs grow rampant around here. No one would pay more than a few coppers for them."

"I'm telling you," Benton said, "you should send one of your girls with the carnival down to Saxbridge for the winter with a crate of these"—he held the vial up to the light —"and they'd have bags of coins upon their return."

Heather held her breath, turning to look at her father. She couldn't imagine he would agree, but how amazing would it be to travel to Saxbridge with the fair?

"I thought the green witches had the south covered," Rose said, setting her jaw to the side.

"Oh they make the revels happen, sure enough, with their fine food and drink, but they have no power to aid when the parties end," Benton said. "Hangover tonics and stomach-settling elixirs are a hot commodity down there if you're a witch worth your salt."

Heather's father cocked his head at Benton, his eyes sliding to Heather for a brief moment. "Something to consider," he murmured. He hadn't dispensed with the idea entirely, but Heather knew from his tone the answer would be no. He wouldn't let his eighteen-year-old daughter travel into the heart of debauchery in a caravan of carnival witches.

"I'll help you carry these, Em," Benton said, shuffling forward to grab one of the packed boxes from the table.

Frowning, Emry looked to Heather. Their excuse to buy themselves a little more time together had been pulled out from under them.

"See you at the fair," Emry said to the room, though Heather knew the red witch spoke directly to her.

Stomach dropping with every step, Heather watched the two carnival witches move out the front door, bracing against the mist of light rain.

A large bag of coins clinked loudly behind her. "500 *druni*," Heather's father said with a loud guffaw. "Can you believe it?"

"I think I like her," Rose said from behind Heather.

Remembering the feeling of Emry's lips, her spicy floral scent, Heather whispered, "Me too."

"But think of how much money we could make," Heather pressed for the hundredth time in the last hour. She and her mother carried armfuls of dried washing in from the line. The morning sun was still low, casting long shadows through the trees. Her siblings were just beginning to stir, but Heather and her mother were awake, the washing an ever-present chore. Soon enough they would have to dry all of their clothes by the fire, the winter sun no longer reliable for the task. It would take twice as long.

"The answer is no, Heather," her mother tutted, pushing open the back door to the shop with her hip. "You are not going to Saxbridge unescorted. You're too young."

"I'm eighteen."

"And you're needed in the shop." Her voice softened as she added, "Your father needs you."

Heather knew her mother worried about her father's health, but her father had been poorly her whole life and he still kept going. It felt like a mean excuse to force her to stay where she was.

"Rose can handle the shop and it's quiet in winter anyway. Plus, I'll only be gone for a couple of months. Father will be fine and I'll come back with bags of gold!"

Her mother spun on her so fast she thought she might collide with her chest. She looked down at Heather with steely blue eyes. Gone was her softness. It was the face that told her children the conversation was over. "Trust that there are some things I know more about than you and this is one of them. No more talk of gallivanting off to Saxbridge. Your family needs you here."

Shoulders slumping, Heather hung her head. Tears pricked her eyes, but she swallowed and they ebbed. She wouldn't cry in front of her mother. Her mother was warm and hard in equal measure, stern but fair, and she couldn't fault her logic this time. It did sound ridiculous: the thought of her moving to the seedy capital city with nothing other than her glass vials.

"Besides, it would not be for only a couple of months," her mother said, more to herself than to Heather as she dumped the washing onto the table and began shaking it out.

That's when Heather knew. Her mother did not fear her going—her mother feared she would never come back. Would a few months with Emry be enough or would she fall even deeper under the red witch's spell? Would the magic of the world bewitch her so much that she would never want to return to Valtene?

Clenching her fists by her side, Heather gritted her teeth, wishing to lash out at her mother but knowing it would only make matters worse. She needed to get out of there before this descended into a shouting match.

"Where are you going?" her mother's taciturn voice called as Heather stormed towards the door.

"Foraging," Heather growled.

"Mm-hmm," her mother hummed in that infuriatingly knowing way—the same way Rose did. "Just be back before lunchtime. We've got harvest moon celebrations to prepare for."

"Yes, Ma," Heather grumbled as she made her way out

the door, her feet steering her in the direction of the fair-grounds through Wyxshire Woods.

Her gut clenched, muscles stiffening, fighting against the angry notion that the following night would be the full moon . . . and that would mean that it was the last night before Emry left. Two more days together—that was all they had.

Pausing on the path, she watched as autumn leaves of brilliant red and orange danced down around her. Should she keep going? She knew every step doomed her to a harder goodbye. Each time she saw Emry, it made it more difficult for her to stay away. Her feet picked up again, her boots crunching leaves the only sound. She had damned herself the moment she saw Emry. It was already too late.

CHAPTER FOUR

The campsite was hushed as the golden sun rose into the trees. Half-assembled stalls and shut wagon doors greeted her as she tiptoed across the grounds. Most of the carnival witches would probably still be asleep, living by the light of the moon, but a line of smoke swirled from the center of the spiral—so Heather knew at least one witch was awake.

Witches weren't completely nocturnal creatures, but they had a predisposition to prefer the night. Even the youngest among them stayed up until midnight. In the summer, they woke long after the rising sun, but in winter, the darkness demanded they wake with the mid-morning star.

Heather rounded the bend, the shimmering gold sun painted on Emry's wagon beckoning her even as she began to second guess arriving in the quiet of the morning. Dew clung to her boots as she moved like a phantom across the fairground. Emry was probably still asleep. She should turn back, but one of the wagon windows was open. Heather peeked inside. The loud caw of the raven made her jolt, her heart skipping a beat in terror. She hadn't noticed Ravi perched on the door.

A head popped up from behind a large stack of crates. Emry's hair was tousled, her face sleepy, tunic unbuttoned in a deep V, but she was fully dressed. Heather released a sigh of relief that she had not woken her up.

"Heather," Emry said in that slow burning way. Tingles danced around Heather's body at her name on Emry's tongue. "Come in."

Nervously chewing her lip, Heather climbed the three steps into the belly of the wagon. The back was crammed with towering crates of witch goods, making an aisle just wide enough for Heather to squeeze through, but beyond the alley of boxes, the wagon opened into a beautiful sitting room. A purple velvet couch sat against one wall, nailed to the wagon's floor. A table and chairs sat beside it, an ornate, colorful rug underneath them. Every inch of space was covered in something: plants, curtains, throw pillows, all in a zany combination of colors and patterns, their vibrancy a perfect match for a carnival witch. The imprint of traveling life was stamped all over the room, from the cabinet of mismatched Southern teacups to the Eastern carved wood windows.

A ladder to the right led up to a loft above the sitting room. Heather saw the edge of a mattress and eiderdown blanket. That must be where Emry slept. It seemed like a cozy nook, one Heather wouldn't mind climbing up to and exploring.

A single cup of inky black tea sat on the table. Heather sniffed the air.

"Your tea smells off," she said, immediately cringing when she realized she'd said it out loud. "I mean . . . this place is beautiful."

"It's coffee," Emry said, chuckling as she moved to her steaming cup. "The green witches of *Carnivale du Fareas* are the best cooks in all the realm. They keep me well-fed and always have a pot of coffee on their fires." She took another step toward Heather, proffering the mug. "Do you want to try some?"

Heather eyed the black liquid before taking the cup. It had a nutty, rich aroma. She raised the mug to her lips, the bitterness of the drink assaulting her taste buds, making her grimace and Emry snort.

"How can you drink that?" Heather's face contorted as she scraped her tongue along the roof of her mouth.

"What can I say? It grows on you." Emry had a hearty, deep laugh that never ceased to bring a smile to Heather's face. She had a terrible urge to run her fingers over the red witch's dimples.

"I think I'll stick to tea," Heather rasped.

"Shall I put the kettle on?" Emry turned to the little black stove in the corner. A thin pipe chimney rose up and out through a hole in the wagon's covered roof.

"No, no, that's fine. I already had a cup this morning," Heather said, shifting on her feet, unsure how to proceed.

Emry smirked at her. "What are you thinking about?"

Heather's pulse quickened as she wrung her hands, but she forced herself to murmur, "If I said I wanted to come with you to Saxbridge, what would you say?"

Emry took a slow step toward Heather, close enough now that the buttons of her tunic brushed against the heavy fabric of Heather's dress. "I'd say that would make me very happy."

Heather's eyes shot up to Emry's. "Really?"

"Really."

"But isn't that insane?" Heather's forehead creased with worry. "We just met each other."

"Yes," Emry said, grinning at Heather's worried expression. She reached out and threaded her fingers through Heather's, the contact lighting up every inch of Heather's body. "And I'd like to get to know you more. Why couldn't we do that on the road?"

"Because what if you get sick of me after three days?" Heather's eyes scanned the room wildly, thinking of every way that choice could go wrong.

"I very much doubt that." Emry huffed. "You might get sick of me."

"I wouldn't." Heather instantly shook her head, and Emry's grin grew as she squeezed their joined hands. Heather looked up at Emry—that smooth skin, those full lips, those piercing brown eyes. Heather jolted away, breaking Emry's hold. "I can't go with you. My parents would never let me go."

She thought of her mother's stern glare and her father's ashen face, regret building in her that she had come to the carnival again.

"Maybe we could talk to them," Emry offered.

"No." Heather ground her teeth, a knot tightening in her throat. "I shouldn't be here."

"If you don't want to see me"—Emry tilted her head— "why do you keep coming back?"

"Because I *do* want to see you, but I can't just go." Heather bit back the tears welling in her eyes. This was not how she'd thought this conversation would go. "My family says they need me."

"Do they?" Emry asked, rubbing her thumb thoughtfully across her bottom lip. "That sister of yours seems to run the show, anyway."

"She does." Heather huffed a laugh. "No, they don't really need me to stay. They are just adamant I shouldn't go." She looked up with heavy, sorrowful eyes. "I could run away—"

"No." Emry shook her head emphatically. "Don't do that to your family."

"Didn't you run away?"

"My family knew I was going, they just disapproved." Emry looked at the opposite wall, her memories taking her far from the wagon. "Red witches can be a stoic lot. Their warmth is skin deep. It's hard to explain."

"I understand," Heather murmured. The red witch coven had always held itself above the rest of the witches, carrying themselves like warriors. Heather could see where Emry got that cool nature from.

"Your family loves you, Heather. You can't just run off in the middle of the night. They would worry themselves sick over you."

Heather hung her head. Emry was right.

"So I either get their blessing or I don't come?" She swallowed the lump in her throat. "Then I won't be coming."

"I'm not saying you need their permission," Emry said, taking a step back to her. "But tell them your decision and be honest with them about it."

Heather bit her lip again, making Emry reach up and skim Heather's mouth with her thumb. Lips parting, Heather stared up at the red witch.

"You leave the day after tomorrow," Heather whispered as her chest seized. "I know that if I never see you again . . . it would break my heart."

Emry's eyes flickered a faint crimson, a sign of deep emotions stirring even if she wished to hide them. Heather was certain her brown magic would be glowing the same. She couldn't believe she had said it, but it was the truth: she'd be heartbroken if Emry disappeared. As suddenly as the red witch became a part of her life, her feelings for Emry weren't fleeting. Somewhere deep in her soul she knew that.

"Come with me to Saxbridge," Emry whispered, voiced tinged with pleading as she cupped Heather's cheek.

Heather's voice shook as she said, "I will."

Emry's lips met Heather's before she could finish her words. Fisting handfuls of Emry's tunic, Heather pulled her closer. It was a desperate kiss, one of sorrow and of hope. Emry's lips promised they would stay together with every burning brush of her mouth.

Heather surrendered to the moment, sliding her hand up Emry's tunic. Her fingers skimmed over her warm, soft skin, making Emry hum. The faint taste of coffee hit Heather's lips as Emry's tongue brushed the seam of her mouth, tongue caressing her own. The feeling made her boneless, like her legs might drop out from under her.

Emry shifted her, moving her toward the velvet couch and holding the back of Heather's neck to guide her down onto the cushions. Heather's hands roved Emry's back as the red witch lowered herself onto Heather. The press of Emry against her made Heather's whole body shudder. The taut muscle of Emrys's thigh settled between Heather's legs, making her shift her hips deeper into the sensation. A deep, sensual laugh escaped Emry's lips as she pressed her leg down harder, making Heather gasp. Emry's fingers reached down to Heather's bare calf. Hiking up her dress with a groan, her hand skimmed up Heather's leg leaving a trail of goosebumps before settling on her hip.

A shrill caw rang out from the back of the wagon.

"Curse the Moon," Emry muttered against Heather's lips. Propping herself up on her elbows she called out, "What is it?"

"The girl's mother is on her way," a deep voice boomed. Heather identified it as belonging to the blue witch fortune teller from the wagon next door.

Heather groaned. Her mother saw through her that easily, knowing exactly where her daughter was heading off to.

"If you keep up with what you're doing, an epic fight will ensue," the fortune teller called in a sing-song way from beyond the stacks of crates.

"Okay, Mallor, thanks," Emry called bitterly. She turned her eyes back to Heather. "What do you want to do?"

"I should go," Heather said. "I need to talk to her."

Emry nodded, brushing her lips across Heather's cheek and up to her ear. "Good luck."

Heather groaned. "Mother Moon, I will need it."

"You'll come back for the celebrations tomorrow?" Emry trailed kisses down Heather's neck, her teeth scraping along her shoulder.

"Yes." Heather let out a hiss of pleasure. "You are making it very hard for me to leave right now."

Emry chuckled, brushing her short hair back off her face, her mussed coif making her look even more stunning. She stood, offering her hand out to help Heather up.

As Heather rose, she keenly yearned for the press of their bodies again. "I'll see you tomorrow," she promised, turning to go, but Emry grabbed her by the crook of the arm and whirled her round. As Emry planted a last kiss on her lips, Heather's head swam, each kiss a brand, a pledge for a future that she had never known she wanted but now was all-consuming.

The harvest moon cast a white glow over the graveyard at the edge of town. It was not quiet and solemn this night, no. On the night of the harvest moon, the burial ground was filled with singing and candlelight.

Despite her promises, Heather hadn't been able to go to the celebrations at the fair that morning. The apothecary was overrun with last-minute shoppers, seeking potions and elixirs to aid them the morning after the revels. The witches would dance and drink and celebrate the last of the sun at the *Carnivale du Fareas*, but once the moon rose into the sky, they would all make their pilgrimage to the graves of their ancestors. Most of Valtene was crammed into the cemetery, prepared to stay all night and keep the waking spirits of their ancestors company.

Heather had managed to skirt around her mother on her path to the fair the day before, avoiding discovery. When her mother returned to the shop, Heather was waiting there with a bundle of fennel. She knew her mother still suspected her of having gone to the fairgrounds, but neither of them was going to say it out loud. It would be just another secret between them.

Each of the Doledirs held a long white candle, standing in a line before the family graves. They all wore long, flowing black robes and black pointed hats—the ceremonial garb of the season, to welcome their ancestors back to the world for one night.

"You see?" Heather's mother murmured to her under the cacophony of chants and cheers. She tilted her pointed hat to the grave in front of them, reading "Adisa Monroe", the name of her mother's great-grandmother.

It was said she was once the most powerful witch in Valtene. She was the creator of the sleeping potion laced with bloodbane that eased the most devastating of injuries.

Heather knew she should be proud of her family's legacy; that tonight when her ancestors' spirits roamed the earth, she should feel some sort of connection to them. But there was only one person she felt connected to, and that person was not here. She had no desire to be the next Adisa Monroe. She did not want to run an apothecary empire or have grand titles bestowed on her while never leaving her little Western town—she wanted to see the world.

"You belong here with your people," her mother said, as if reading her mind. "And when your father and I go"—she shot a quick sorrowful look at Heather's father—"you will still be able to be with us."

"It will be a long time before you or father go," Heather reassured her mother.

Ma's face cracked for a moment, her calm matronly mask slipping, revealing the grief that hid underneath it. "You are wrong, my love," she whispered, her voice breaking as she wrapped her arm around Heather's shoulders.

"No," Heather gasped, stealing a glance at her father who was hugging Oliver around the shoulders.

"He did not want to scare you," Ma murmured. "But you are old enough now to know the truth. I fear if you go he will not be here when you return."

The truth laid bare, she finally understood why her mother turned so severe every time she discussed leaving.

Her mother had held tight to the secret that her father's health was indeed declining. The warmth seemed to bleed from Ma, the sharpness hiding a deeper sorrow. Heather had thought he would go on that way forever, sickly but strong. Racing through her memories of the past years, she tried to pinpoint when it took a turn for the worse. Guilt coursed through her for not having seen it, too focused on herself. She wondered how long her parents had known. How long had they worn those masks of bravery for their children?

"I'm sorry, Ma," Heather choked out, trying to hide her emotions as Rose looked their way.

The Creighton Family behind them burst into uproarious song again, swaying as they serenaded their ancestors with a drunken ballad. Rose turned to scowl at them.

"Can we go say our prayers now?" Rose asked, turning to their father. She didn't even have to crane her neck to look at him from under the brim of her hat. At sixteen, she was already his height.

"Yes, go find a quiet spot. We'll meet back here in an hour," he said with a soft smile. They would spend all night around this graveyard. Her mother had packed a basket of food and blankets. They would stay with their ancestors until the sun rose and their spirits lay back to rest. "Moon Blessings."

"Moon Blessings," Ma echoed to a passing family, her expression merry once more, but Heather knew the sadness that lay underneath it.

The Doledir children scattered in every direction, Heather roving farther through the edge of the woods, downhill, until she was out of sight, giving her a moment to breathe.

She stooped, pushing her finger into the frigid earth and

making a hole to hold her candle straight. Pulling her thick robes underneath her, she sat, protecting her body from the cold ground. Removing her hat, she pulled the strings of her totem bag from around her neck, opening the small black pouch.

The totems clinked in a familiar, comforting sound as she moved the bag. One by one, she laid out her totems to bathe in the moonlight: a smooth white river stone, a blue glass marble, a thimble, a piece of lizard skin, and a sprig of dried lavender. She pulled the lavender out of the line, tossed it into the forest, and grabbed a burgundy leaf to replace it. Some totems she would keep forever, and others were only meant for one moon cycle. She would carry this leaf for the next moon cycle and then trade it for a new one.

Striking the flint from her bag, she lit her candle. "Mother Moon, bless me this night." The practiced words tumbled from her mouth, having heard them uttered every full moon of her entire life. Silence greeted her as she waited for a glimmer of intuition to pop into her mind—a resolution for the next moon cycle.

On the harvest moon, the voices of her ancestors could whisper through the fires. She stared at the deep blue belly of the flame, waiting to hear any voices that might murmur into her mind. But she couldn't wait, already knowing the truth from the moment she set her candle in the earth.

"I need to stay, don't I?" Heather's chest constricted as though a fist clenched in the center of her sternum. She raged at herself. That was her first thought? She didn't worry first about her ailing father or her heartbroken mother —she worried for herself.

She scowled at the ground.

"If something happens to Father while I'm gone . . . I

need to be here, lot of good I would do them, but"—Heather hung her head in her hands—"I can't just go."

A memory flickered into Heather's mind. She was a child sitting on her grandmother's lap. "I would gladly give my life for those I love," her grandmother said with a hearty witch's cackle, kissing the top of Heather's young head.

She remembered that day. It had been the Winter Solstice and she had spent the morning building snow forts with Rose and Cole. Her mother had watched from the window, her belly swollen with Evelyn. Their grandparents had lived with them then, in the room that had since become her brother's bedroom. Heather, Rose, and Cole had all shared a bed. She still could remember the excitement—to have a whole day spent playing with new toys and eating a hearty winter feast. She never felt more like a family then on those days, the bonds between them like a living thread tying them together.

Her grandmother was right. Even her ancestors were warning her away from her doomed plan. Family was the most important thing. She should give her life, her happiness, to stay with them.

Tears welled in Heather's eyes. She blinked them down her cheeks as she placed her totems back in her bag.

She held her intention for the month ahead in her mind's eye. She would focus on being a better daughter, a more dutiful shop worker, and a more responsible elder sister. She envisioned the version of herself she wanted to be—graceful, calm in crisis, and hard-working.

Her voice wobbled as she whispered to the candle, "This or something better now manifests for the highest good of all." She blew it out, magic swirling in the smoke of the blackened wick. The resolve of her intention did nothing to soften her pain.

Her choice was made.

She crumpled forward, hiding her tear-streaked face in her hands. She would have to say goodbye to Emry and to her dreams of leaving this town. She prayed that the desire to join Emry would leave as swiftly as it came.

Sliding the string of her totem bag back over her head, she grabbed her candle and pointed hat. As she stood, her eyes snagged on a shadowed figure standing underneath an elm tree, watching her. The figure's hands and face glowed a faint red, snuffing out as Heather turned. Her stomach lurched. She had to end it now.

She wrung her hat in her hands as she walked farther from the graveyard toward Emry. The red witch looked stunning decked out in her ceremonial witch's garb, her short curls swooped to one side, her black robes shimmering with iridescence like a raven's wing.

Grief peeked out from behind the red witch's stoic mask, her eyes flashing crimson as she struggled to contain it. Heather was sure she was glowing as well, although the brown witches' magic was such a faint color it was often missed in the darkness.

Emry reached out a finger and swiped away Heather's tear, the action causing more tears to instantly appear.

"You're not coming, are you?" Emry's voice was scratchy and rough, as though she had been screaming.

"I can't leave my family," Heather whispered as she bit back her tears. "My father is not well and I—"

Emry swallowed, voice clipped as she said, "I understand."

"I was being selfish thinking I could just leave," Heather sputtered, desperate to explain herself. "You should be relieved. After all, we just met, who knows if—"

"Stop," Emry growled, looking up as her eyes flared.

"This is your life. These are your choices. But don't ask me to hide my disappointment, because I can't."

Heather bit the inside of her cheek. "I'm sorry."

Emry reached out, wrapping her hand slowly around the back of Heather's neck as she said, "I don't want to say goodbye."

"Neither do I." Heather's voice cracked as the tears rushed down her face again.

The slightest pressure of Emry's fingertips on her neck had them both moving, their mouths colliding in a burning, impassioned kiss. Heather whimpered, arms enveloping Emry's hard back to pull her tighter against her. The knot in her chest clenched so tightly she couldn't breathe. She wanted to fuse their hearts together so that they would never be apart again. Yearning rose in her like a white hot flame. She could taste the salt of her tears on Emry's tongue, their longing kiss tinged with frustration at the life they could not have.

Emry broke away all at once, leaving Heather cold.

"I have to go," Emry said, a haunted look on her face as she touched her fingers to her bruised lips. "If I stay with you tonight, saying goodbye tomorrow . . . I don't think I can survive it."

Heather took a jagged breath, feeling like she was shattering into a hundred pieces at that admission. Emry reached into her tunic. Pulling on the strings of her totem bag, she reached in and produced a shimmering golden stone.

"So you can keep the sunshine with you this winter," she said, taking Heather's hand and placing the citrine in her palm. As she closed Heather's fingers around the stone, her eyes flared such a brilliant scarlet that it lit up the night.

"Goodbye, Heather," she said, and walked away before Heather could reply.

Heather let out a silent sob, turning back toward the main road. She would not be returning to the graveyard. She needed to cry her heart out alone.

CHAPTER FIVE

She made it to the back gate of the shop before halting in the leaves, sobs shaking her whole body. She could barely take a breath, wringing out the sorrow possessing her body. In the far reaches of her mind, she could hear her parents admonishing her for this overreaction, but her legs refused to move. The grief took control of her body as she clutched the golden stone to her chest.

Collapsing against the gate, Heather bawled for hours. The cold night air seeped into her body, her limbs heavy with exhaustion, wearier than if she had climbed a mountain. The wind through the naked trees grew silent in the predawn forest, the stillness signaling the coming of the sun. Heather knew she should get back to the graveyard before her family left. There would be more singing and farewelling their ancestors before the drowsy townsfolk returned to their beds. They would sleep the day away while the carnival rolled out of town.

Hauling her body up from beside the gate, Heather's eyes snagged on the flickering of a candle. Someone was in the shop.

She pushed through the back gate and into the kitchen. Sure enough, the candle on the mantle was gone and the faint glow of light came from the front of the apothecary. Heather's eyes widened, wondering if it was a thief. She should probably run back to the graveyard and tell her family rather than confront the burglar, but by then they might be gone.

Her hands roved over the sharp kitchen knives for a moment before she thought better of it. She couldn't just stab someone with a carving knife. Rose probably could. Instead, she grabbed the rolling pin and tiptoed toward the front of the shop.

"Gah!" her father exclaimed as she turned the corner, wielding the rolling pin. "What in the Moon's ti—"

Heather barked out a laugh, having never heard him curse before. She eyed the worn leather pack on the countertop. It was a traveler's pack with shoulder straps and compartments. Her father stuffed baskets of herbs and glass vials into the pack until it was nearly full.

"I was about to come find you," he said to Heather, arching his brow.

She knew he could see her tear-stained cheeks. Her eyes were probably red and her countenance raw. "I'm tired. I'm going to bed," she said, rubbing the center of her chest as if it could remove the heartache. "What are you doing here?"

"Packing."

"Packing what?"

Her father peeked up at her over his golden spectacles. "Packing your apothecary bag for when you're on the road."

Heather's heart leapt into her throat. "Wh-what about the shop?"

"Rose can run the shop." Her father waved away her

objection as he buckled the pack closed. "It has been her desire to run this place her whole life."

"And what about you?" Heather asked, scanning her father's gaunt face.

"I will be alright," he said gently. "I will be here."

"No, you won't," Heather said, choking back the tears welling again.

Her father came around the countertop and pulled her into a tight hug. The feeling of his arms, his scent of ink and herbs, felt so familiar and comforting. She wished she could bottle up the warmth of his love and take it with her always.

"I will be here, Heather," he murmured into her hair. "You may only be able to talk to me on the harvest moon but I will always be here."

Heather couldn't believe it was really true, couldn't fathom that he would ever be gone. "But I heard Grandmother's whispers this night. She said 'I would gladly give my life for those I love.' I am meant to stay here."

"You cannot live your whole life waiting for me to die, circling me like a buzzard." Her father released her with a forced laugh. "It will not change anything. It will only make you sadder. I have spoken to my mother this night too, and she has told me the same thing. I think I understand her meaning better than you. You were not meant to stay in Valtene your whole life." Her father gripped her shoulders lightly, peering down into her watery eyes. "I would gladly sacrifice for those I love, Heather."

Hot tears slipped down her cheeks as she sniffled. "But what about—"

"I will handle Ma," he said, already knowing what she feared as he pulled her back into a hug.

"I can't leave without saying goodbye to the others." Her chest seized. How long would it be before she saw her siblings again? A season? A year? "They will never forgive me for disappearing in the night on them." Her mind whirled as her pulse drummed in her ears.

"I will talk to them. They will understand," he said in a warm hush. He lifted the pack off the table and put it on her shoulders. "But you must make haste. The caravan is leaving with the dawn."

"My clothes?" she said, peering up to the ceiling.

"I put the clothes from your drawer in the bag and that book from your bedside table. Whatever else you need you can buy along the way with the *druni* in the front pocket." He brushed a tear off her cheek.

"I love you," Heather whispered, gripping her father in one last fierce hug, a hug she knew somewhere deep in her soul would be their last.

"I love you too," he chuckled softly. "Write me letters so I may hear of all your travels." Heather nodded into his chest, memorizing his scent, his warmth, and the sound of his voice. "Now go have an adventure."

Heather pressed her lips tightly together as she stepped away from him, turning to the front door. A muffled mewl greeted her as Raven jumped onto the table by the door, a dead mouse in her mouth.

"Well done," Heather whispered, giving the cat one last scratch. "You take care of everyone."

She took two *druni* out of her pocket and left them on the table next to Raven, a witch's goodbye. Heather took a steadying breath and stepped out into the early morning light.

Her pulse raced again as she looked up at the sky. The sun was rising. The carnival would be leaving town at any moment. Heather broke into a sprint toward Wyxshire Wood.

The heavy pack slammed against her shoulders as Heather sped through the quiet forest, dashing from stone-to-stone as she cut through the swamp and back up to higher ground. She would have bruises all over her back. She dragged puffs of cold air across her teeth as she willed her legs faster. Leaping over exposed roots and darting under low-hanging branches, she bolted like the Goddess of Death was chasing her.

When she reached the clearing, her heart sank. The spiral of wagons was gone.

The faint shimmer of the rainbow caravan caught the light on the last hill. They were already on the move, too far for Heather to catch up, and yet she did not stop running. Crazed by a desire to not lose sight of the caravan, she dashed through the tall grasses whipping at her legs. She would chase them through the day if she had to. She would follow their trail until she found them. She did not care what it took. She would never be that crumpled girl against the gate again. This was the life she wanted, and she would run it down.

Every time she thought she was gaining on them, the caravan would lurch ahead. Her desperate shouts were lost in the wind. No one would hear her. She spotted the back of the midnight blue wagon as it turned around the bend, the golden bursting sun painted across its side. Her legs burned, her limbs weighted down with lead, but still she did not pause.

The cerulean wagon in front of the midnight one abruptly halted. Heather's heart pounded against her chest as she seized the opportunity to catch them up. She could make out the shape of the blue witch fortune teller as he clambered down from the front of his wagon, waving at the line behind him to wait. He moved to his back wheel, inspecting it.

Heather raced across the field and up onto the wagon trail, darting past the last four wagons, their drivers all looking down at her with amusement.

"What's going on?" Heather knew the voice that called down to the blue witch. "Is your wheel broken?"

As Heather closed the gap, finally slowing her pace, she heaved in great gasps of air.

"Ah no, it was just a mistake . . . the wheel's fine." The stout blue witch looked up at her and gave her a wink.

Heather's face split into a broad smile at him as she finally reached the driver's seat. An ear-splitting caw announced her arrival. Raven sat perched on the top of the wagon.

Emry's eyes flared a brilliant red as soon as they landed on Heather, all the proof Heather needed that Emry's feelings matched her own, as if her heart were exploding from her chest. The red witch was frozen, regarding her with a mixture of awe and disbelief.

Heather swallowed the thick knot in her throat. "Hi," she panted, shucking off her pack with a confidence she had never known before and placing it in the footwell below the bench where Emry sat.

"Hi." Emry smirked, reaching her hand down to help Heather up onto the seat beside her. Emry practically lifted her straight up into the air, the eagerness to get her on board all too apparent. Heather plonked down on the seat as Emry wrapped her arm tightly around Heather's shoulder, kissing her temple.

The blue witch wagon in front of them jolted back to life. Emry turned her twinkling eyes to Heather.

"Ready?" she asked, her eyes hot with emotion as they

roved Heather's face. Heather nodded, and with a flick of the reins, the wagon rocked forward down the bumpy path.

She squinted back toward Valtene as the morning sun warmed her cheeks, a silent goodbye whispering from her heart to her hometown. The Doledir family would be okay without her, she assured herself, as the sunlight gleamed into her eyes. She'd send letters and trinkets back to them in the traveling post. Nerves twisted in her gut. It was thrilling and terrifying all at once. As the wagons rolled beyond the town line, she shook her head in disbelief. She was already the farthest she'd ever been from home.

Emry's hand squeezed her shoulder and she pressed in tighter to the red witch's side. She prayed she could coax this beautiful ember between them into a flame. She thanked Mother Moon that she was even given a chance to try. With each rock and sway of the wagon, the dreams of endless adventures stretched out before her. She wrapped her arm around Emry's back as stray strands of her hair waved in the wind. Raven cawed overhead, flaring his wings to catch the breeze, and in that moment, Heather swore her soul was flying too.

I hope you enjoyed Heather's story! For even more stories around Okrith, check out my Patreon! If you enjoyed reading this story, please consider leaving a review, sharing on social media, or telling a friend! -A.K. xx

Join A. K. Mulford's Patreon to receive ARCs, book mail, access to the Mountaineers discord server, spicy artwork, and brand new novellas!

ACKNOWLEDGMENTS

Thank you to my marvelous alpha readers for your feedback and helping this story take shape and to the Booktok community for all of the support and love. I can't wait to take you on many more journeys to Okrith.

Thank you to Erin from The Word Faery for your impeccable editing services.

Thank you to Norma from Norma's Nook Proofreading, it is always a joy to work with you.

Thank you to Holly Dunn for designing the map of Okrith and to MiblArt for the cover design.

ABOUT THE AUTHOR

A.K. Mulford is a bestselling fantasy author and former wildlife biologist who swapped rehabilitating monkeys for writing novels.

She/they are inspired to create diverse stories that transport readers to new realms, making them fall in love with fantasy for the first time, or, all over again.

She now lives in Australia with her husband and two young human primates, creating lovable fantasy characters and making ridiculous Tiktok videos.

www.akmulford.com

The Okrith Novellas

The Witch of Crimson Arrows

The Witch Apothecary

The Witchslayer

The Witching Trail

The Witch's Goodbye

The Five Crowns Of Okrith Series

The High Mountain Court

The Witches' Blade

The Rogue Crown

The Evergreen Heir

The Amethyst Kingdom

The Golden Court Series

A River of Golden Bones

A Sky of Emerald Stars